I'M <u>NOT</u> SCARED... I'M PREPARED!

BECAUSE I KNOW ALL ABOUT ALICE

TRAINING INSTITUTE

Alert
Lockdown
Inform
Counter
Evacuate

The gift of Being Prepared

published by

National Center for Youth Issues

Practical Guidance Resources
Educators Can Trust

ncyi.org

www.ncyi.org

Forward

The world will forever remember December 14th, 2012...the day 26 angels from Sandy Hook Elementary were created. The outpouring of support for all those affected by this tragedy is evidence that our world is still full of more good than evil. It also affirms our mission of the ALICE Training Institute: To remain steadfast in striving to keep our schools safe.

We must expand school safety programs and empower schools, parents, teachers and students with multiple options on how to respond during the invasion of a violent intruder. The US Department of Education now recommends such practices as described in its School Emergency Operation Plan (June 2013.)

> *"As the situation develops, it is possible that students and staff will need to use more than one option...
> often they will have to rely on their own judgment to decide which option will best protect lives."*

Julia Cook does a masterful job in presenting the ALICE curriculum (used in schools and universities nation-wide) in an age-appropriate manner. This book provides the missing piece to the puzzle, linking crucial safety information into the world view of elementary aged children in a powerful and proactive way.

A portion of the proceeds of this book will proudly be donated to non-profit organizations whose missions include school safety and empowering community involvement (parents, educators, first responders, and mental health professionals) to improve school safety.

For more information about the ALICE Training Institute and the wonderful organizations that it helps support, go to www.AliceTraining.com

Greg Crane
Founder/President of the ALICE Training Institute

A NOTE TO THE READER

The information contained in this book is meant to supplement active shooter response protocols that appear in a school's Emergency Operation Plan (EOP) and are therefore provided 'as is' without warranty of any kind, neither implied nor express, including but not limited to implied warranties of suitability for a particular purpose.

National Center for Youth Issues, the ALICE Training Institute, the writers, editors, illustrators and designers of this work shall in no event be liable for any damages or losses including, without limitation, direct, indirect, special, punitive, incidental or consequential damages resulting from or caused by this book or its content, including without limitation, any error, omission, or defect. In any event, liability shall not exceed the retail price, or any lesser amount, actually paid for the purchase of this book.

ADDITIONAL RESOURCES

U.S. Department of Education, et al. 2013. *Guide for Developing High-quality School Emergency Operations Plans.* http://rems.ed.gov

International Association of Chiefs of Police, 2009. *Guide for Preventing & Responding to School Violence.* http://www.theiacp.org/Prevention-And-Response-To-School-Violence

Federal Emergency Management Agency (FEMA) Training. IS-100. SCA: *Introduction to the Incident Command Systems for Schools.* http://www.fema.gov/national-incident-management-system

National Center for Youth Issues
Practical Guidance Resources Educators Can Trust
ncyi.org

P.O. Box 22185
Chattanooga, TN 37422-2185
423.899.5714 • 800.477.8277
fax: 423.899.4547 • www.ncyi.org

ISBN: 978-1-937870-28-7
© 2014 National Center for Youth Issues, Chattanooga, TN
All rights reserved.
Written by: Julia Cook
Illustrations by: Michelle Hazelwood Hyde
Design by: Phillip W. Rodgers
Contributing Editor: Beth Spencer Rabon
Published by National Center for Youth Issues • Softcover
Printed at Starkey Printing, Chattanooga, Tennessee, U.S.A., April 2014

I'm an ant.

I go to the school that's up on the hill...
That's why they call it the Ant Hill School!

My teacher's the BEST! She cares about every single ant in my class! She always says:

"The very best gifts that I can give to each and every one of you, are the gifts of being prepared...for EVERYTHING!"

But sometimes, I think she gives out **waayyyyy** too many gifts!

4

My teacher never wants anything bad to happen to us, so she is always trying to figure out the best ways to keep us safe.

- "Look both ways twice before you cross, and always watch where you are going!"

- "Make sure your hands are germ-free before you eat lunch!"

- "Please walk in the hallway...don't run, and watch where you're going!"

- "Try to remember not to lean back in your chair!"

We even have safety drills that we practice.

There's the Fire Drill, so we'll be prepared and know what to do if we ever have a fire.

There's the Bad Weather Drill, so we'll be prepared and know what to do if we ever have bad weather.

And today, my teacher taught us a new drill. It's called **The Sheep, The Shepherd, and the Wolf Drill**. This is the drill that teaches us what to do if there is ever a "dangerous someone" inside our school that isn't supposed to be there.

Great plan of action =
ALICE

"Class, my teacher said to us, we need to learn a new drill.
It's called The Sheep, The Shepherd and the Wolf,
so get ready...here's the deal!"

"I'll be your shepherd, and you're all my sheep,
so you must do what I say.
Pretend there's a wolf in our building, and we MUST stay out of his way!"

"We need a great plan of action in case we start to get scared.
The A.L.I.C.E. Plan will work the best, to help us be prepared."

The

"A" stands for ALERT. (There's a wolf in the building!)

"L" says we need to LOCK DOWN.

"I" says INFORM, 'cause we must tell others if we've seen the wolf around.

"C" stands for COUNTER. If the wolf sees us, we must do things to ruin his day.

"E" stands for EVACUATE, which means leave the building and run away!"

"But where do we run? I asked, and when do we stop?"

"Excellent question, my teacher said. Let's all take a walk and I'll show you."

"See this great big tree that's two blocks away from school? You need to run until you get to this tree. And then you need to **STOP**. This will be our special meeting place!"

Go Me!

We all walked back to our classroom and sat in our seats, and then my teacher said:

"Sheep, Shepherd, Wolf is an important drill, but there's no reason for you to feel scared. You have ME for a teacher! And I'll make sure that you are prepared."

"Here's how it works."

"When I give you the signal for Sheep, Shepherd, Wolf,

STOP, LOOK and LISTEN to me.

When I give you directions, don't ask me WHY?

Just get to where you're supposed to be."

"I am your shepherd, and you are my sheep,
and you need to do what I say.

There's a wolf in the building...**a dangerous someone**,
and we need to stay out of his way!"

"If we need to go into LOCK DOWN, we get quiet and stay out of sight.
But we don't try to hide in the closet, or squish together too close and tight."

"We need to be ready to move and spread out, so don't all stand in a clump.
Have enough space to move your arms in a circle, and get your legs ready to JUMP!"

"We must do what we can to INFORM the others, by telling them all that we know.

Then look around and find a **something** to hold onto, something that's easy to throw."

"A shoe from a cubby, a block of wood, or maybe a TV remote,

A paper-back book, a video game, or even a plastic goat!"

"If the wolf gets into our classroom,
we'll know just what to do.

Make noise, run around and
throw our **somethings** at the wolf,
and then we'll run right through,

the door and down the hallway, but don't run in a straight line.
Run in a funny ZiG-ZAGGY way, and make strange noises the whole time!

14

"You want us to RUN in the HALLWAY?" I asked.

"It's always OK to run in halls when you are practicing the SHEEP, SHEPHERD, WOLF drill....but,

"Make sure you are careful when you run ZIG-ZAGG
and don't run into each other.

Instead, keep an eye out for those around you,
and try to help one another.

Waive your hands in the air, and act kinda strange,
then outside the door we will go.

Then run and run as fast as you can,
'til we get to that tree that we know.

Don't wait for me
to run to the tree.

Just do what you
already know.

Run and run
as fast as you can.

Get ready, Get Set...

GO!

"You might run faster
than I do,
and you might
beat me to the tree.

But that's OK,
'cause you did what I said,
and I know that you
listened to me."

EXIT

"There may be other times during LOCK DOWN when we don't stay in our classroom and wait.

I may help you climb out the first floor window, then run to the tree that's so great!

You just never know when we play Sheep, Shepherd, Wolf what your instructions are going to be.

You MUST remember to STOP, LOOK and LISTEN, 'cause we'll need to move QUICKLY!"

Fire Drill

Bad Weather

18

"Now, let's practice!

I've asked our custodian, Mr. Olsen, to be the wolf. I even have a wolf outfit for Mr. Olsen to wear!"

19

Our teacher gave us the signal
for The Sheep, The Shepherd
and The Wolf Drill, and we

STOPPED, LOOKED and LISTENED,

and then did exactly
what she told us to do.

First, she helped all of us climb out of the
window. Then we ran as fast as we could until
we got to the great big tree that's two blocks
away. Then we stopped. I ran so fast that I
beat my teacher to the tree!

Then, we all walked back
to school, went back
into our classrooms and
practiced some more.

She gave us the SHEEP, SHEPHERD, WOLF signal again and we STOPPED, LOOKED and LISTENED, and then did exactly what she told us to do.

Our teacher locked the door. Then we all helped her push the tables in front of the door. She tied one of the table legs to the door knob with a jump rope, while we all quietly grabbed our **somethings**, spread out, and stayed out of sight.

My **something** was a plastic camel...I couldn't find the goat.

Our teacher locked the door,
and put a belt around the
arm thingie at the top.

Mr. Olsen somehow figured out
how to get into our classroom,
but when he opened the door,
we were ready for him.

**We all jumped
up QUICKLY!**

But instead of throwing our **somethings** at Mr. Olsen, we threw wadded up paper balls at him. They don't hurt as much when they hit you, and like my teacher always says: "Safety drills are supposed to help us NOT hurt us!"

We made it through the doorway,

and ran ZiG-ZAGGY down the hall,

waiving our arms in the air and making really strange noises.

We were **super** careful not to run into each other.

Then, we ran outside and kept running as fast as we could until we got to the great big, huge tree. And then we stopped.
This time, almost everybody beat my teacher!

When she made it to the tree, she gave us all a big hug and told us that we were the BEST LISTENERS EVER!

"We must remember to STOP, LOOK and LISTEN whenever we have a drill. Sheep always do what the shepherd says, regardless of how they feel."

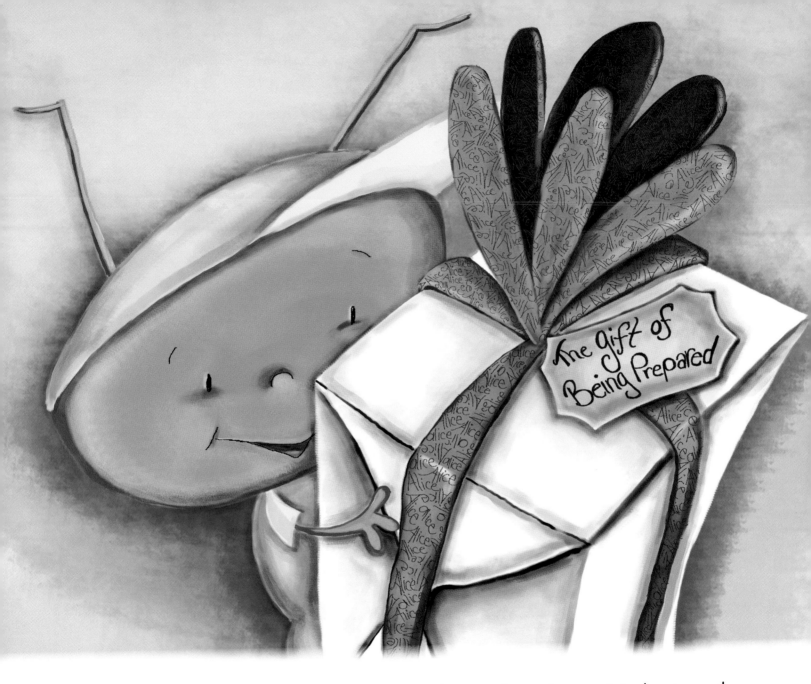

My teacher gave us a great gift today, and she taught us how not to be scared. There are wolves in our world, but we know what to do, and now we are **PREPARED!**"

When I got home from school,
my mom asked me what I did today...
so I told her the truth...

"I learned all about **ALiCE**,
climbed out of a window and
ran to the great, big tree twice.

I threw paper wad balls at Mr. Olsen,
and I wasn't supposed to be nice!

I ran **ZiG-ZAGGY** down the hallway,

and made strange noises
with my hands in the air.

I did all of these things at school today Mom, and my principal didn't even care!"

"YOU DID WHAT????????"

So then, I told my mom what really happened!

"A stands for ALERT. (There's a wolf in the building!)

L says we need to LOCK DOWN.

I says INFORM, 'cause we must tell others if we've seen the wolf around.

C stands for COUNTER. If the wolf sees us, we must do things to ruin his day.

E stands for EVACUATE, which means leave the building and run away!"

A NOTE TO PARENTS AND EDUCATORS

ALICE
TRAINING INSTITUTE | Alert
Lockdown
Inform
Counter
Evacuate

The purpose of this book is to enhance the concepts taught by the ALICE Training Institute and make them applicable to children of all ages in a non-fearful way. By using this book, children can develop a better understanding of what needs to be done if they ever encounter a "dangerous someone." Unfortunately in the world we now live in, we all must ask ourselves the essential question: What options do I have for survival, if I ever find myself in a violent intruder event?

10 Concepts of ALICE for Elementary

ALICE Training for the elementary aged child is age and ability appropriate. **ALICE Training Institute always leaves the grade level of implementation up to the local school district.**

1. Children should be taught to follow direction the first time they are given in an emergency. We don't want teachers to give directions for evacuate or lockdown and have students standing around asking, "But why?"

2. Students should be trained to **STOP, LOOK and LISTEN** to announcements at the time they are given. If the PA system serves as the main information source in a school, students must be trained to **STOP, LOOK and LISTEN** every time it comes on.

3. In a lockdown, be quiet, listen to directions, stay out of the line of sight from the door, but **DO NOT** hide in a closet. Be ready to move or evacuate if the intruder comes into the room.

4. In a counter situation when the secured location has been breached by an intruder, and evacuation is not possible, the best line of defense is to have kids up, moving, making noise, gaining distance and throwing items at the intruder.

5. Evacuation is **always** the best defense, if the information indicates it is safe to do so. Parents, staff and students must know where the RALLY/REUNIFICATION point is located. This

location is usually away and separate from the school. Students should know how to get to the RALLY/REUNIFICATION point from every part of the school, and how to move quickly **with OR without** the teacher. It should be emphasized to parents that the RALLY/REUNIFICATION point is the place to go in case of an emergency.

6. Upper elementary students have more developed critical thinking and problem solving skills and should take a much more active role in ALICE than children in the lower elementary grades.

7. We teach all aspects of ALICE **<u>EXCEPT</u>** the "swarm technique" (grabbing onto the appendages of an intruder and using your body weight to immobilize him) to elementary students.

8. Special needs students are planned for ahead of time, given their individualized situations. If a student cannot evacuate, plans must be made to fortify his/her location. When students with special needs are included in the general education class, teachers need to decide what is in the child's best interest and plans should be made ahead of time. We cannot give a *one-size-fits-all* answer to the situations involving a student with special needs. The school must consider each case individually.

9. Education and empowerment are the keys to preparation and relieving fear.

10. Kids are taught in realistic terms what to do in case of danger. ALICE is much like a fire drill or a tornado drill. Its purpose is to prepare students for life inside and out of the classroom. The ALICE concepts are the same at school, home, the mall, the afterschool program, restaurants, church or any other place the child goes. We are teaching a life-long safety skill.

Alert
Lockdown
Inform
Counter
Evacuate

alicetraining.com

In a moment of decision, the best thing you can do is the right thing. The next best thing is the wrong thing. The worst thing you can do is nothing.

– Theodore Roosevelt